Saved

by

Eleanor Updale

24th November 2008
54050000307405

First published in 2008 in Great Britain by
Barrington Stoke Ltd
18 Walker Street, Edinburgh, EH3 7LP

www.barringtonstoke.co.uk

ISBN: 978-1-84299-526-6

Printed in Great Britain by Bell & Bain Ltd

A Note from the Author

I often go to meetings at a big London hospital. We discuss all sorts of problems that worry the staff and patients. I would never use a real case in my books, but some of the things I have heard about over the years have given me ideas. I have also visited America, and met people with extreme religious views. That made me wonder what happens when children start to question their parents' beliefs.

Saved is not a true story, but the events here could happen, I'm sure.

For Jim, Andrew, Catherine and Flora

Contents

Chapter 1
Crash

Luke was upstairs in his room doing his revision when he heard the crash. It wasn't just one bump, but lots of squeals and thumps. He ran to the window and looked down on the mangled cars below.

There was a taxi, with a huge dent in one side. A white van was crushed against a lamp-post, its front bent in by the impact. In the dark, the street-light was sparking, so that the crash scene was lit up every few moments. On the other side of the road, a lorry had hit a line of parked cars. They had smashed into each other, and one car had risen up and ridden over the roof of another. A red Mini was lying on its side on the pavement.

Luke had never been so excited.

A crash. A real crash. In his street. In boring old Barton Road.

But then Luke saw the people. The back door of the taxi opened, and a woman stepped out, holding one hand to her head. Blood was oozing between her fingers and along the sleeve of her pale jacket.

The taxi driver didn't look hurt, but he was shouting something as he rushed across towards the lamp-post. "I'll kill yer. I'll effing kill yer!" he yelled. Then he stopped in front of the van and saw the driver's limp body lying across the bonnet, covered in broken glass from the windscreen.

Looking down from his room, Luke could tell that the man was already dead.

He looked away, trying to get the picture out of his mind. Across the road, the jumbled cars were like toys kicked aside by an angry child. The Mini seemed to have landed on top of a doll. Luke could see its floppy arms and legs sticking out from under the car.

But it wasn't a doll. He knew that, even though he didn't want to believe it. And he'd seen the shoes before. They were the sensible sandals his sister Anna wore. Their mother always said that anything more modern would be bad for the feet. It was just as well that Luke and Anna were educated at home by their parents. Anna would have been teased if she went to school. No other 13-year-old wore flat shoes with round toes and big buckles.

It must be Anna lying there, crushed under the Mini.

Luke had to get to her.

But it wasn't going to be easy. His parents were out at a church meeting, and they had done what they always did when they left him at home alone. They had locked the front door. They didn't want Luke to go out or, worse still, to let someone in. Nothing should stop him from revising for his mock GCSEs. Even Anna was sent to study at the library. She must have got back early. She must have been waiting for her parents to arrive with the keys when the Mini rode up onto the pavement and hit her.

Luke rushed down-stairs to the kitchen for the phone. But the hand-set was not there. His father had locked it in the medicine cabinet before he left for church. There was no medicine in that cabinet. Just things Luke's parents wanted to keep away from their children: the phone, matches, the power lead from the radio, the aerial wire for the TV.

Luke's parents didn't believe in medicine, but they did believe in evil. And the phone, TV and radio could be evil. Since meeting Pastor David at the Church of the Healer's Message, they saw it as their duty to protect their children from such things.

Luke tried pulling at the door of the cabinet, but it wouldn't open. He ran to the front and back doors. Both were locked. He knew the windows had been painted shut long ago. There was no point trying to open them, so he picked up a chair and threw it through the glass. He climbed out into the front garden, cutting his hand on the way.

Chapter 2
Trapped

The street had begun to fill with people from nearby houses. Several were using mobile phones to call for help. There was a small crowd round the Mini, shouting about what to do.

"We could lift it off her, if we all pulled at once," said one man.

Another said that was wrong. "You'll only injure her more if you do," he said. "We mustn't move her."

"Wait for the ambulance," said a woman.

"We'll need the fire brigade," said another. "She's completely trapped."

Luke had seen all the people in the group before, but he had never spoken to any of them. His parents didn't allow him to mix with the locals. Even so, everyone knew who he was. He was the boy from the strange family who kept themselves to themselves.

One of the women put an arm round him. It felt odd. He wasn't used to being touched. "It's your sister, dear. She'll be OK, I'm sure."

Luke could tell that she didn't really mean it.

A man was talking to Anna. "She can't hear me, but she's still breathing," he said.

Luke could hear sirens far away. After a long wait, an ambulance arrived, closely followed by two fire engines and several police cars. Blue flashes joined the flickering lamp-light. Nothing seemed real to Luke. It was like being in a film, or a worn-out video that wasn't playing properly.

All the time, he was thinking of what his parents would say. He knew they would want him to stop anyone taking Anna to hospital.

A large fireman took control. "Move back, everyone. Move away. There's nothing to see here."

Of course, there was a lot to see – the crowd, the blood, the twisted metal – but, most important of all, the struggle to get Anna out from under the Mini. A police-woman took Luke to one side and wrote down his name, Anna's name, and their address. Luke pointed to his house, just across the road.

"And you were in there on your own?" said the police-woman.

"I'm 15," said Luke. "It's allowed, isn't it?"

"Yes, dear," said the police-woman, kindly. "I was just thinking about how we might get hold of your parents."

"They're at church," said Luke.

The police-woman pointed down the hill. "That one there?" she asked. "St Mary's?"

Luke suddenly felt embarrassed. "No. It's a different church. A special one. On the other side of town, the Church of the Healer's Message."

"I don't know that church," said the police-woman, trying to smile. "But we'll find them. You can go with Anna in the ambulance, and we'll send a car to bring them on to the hospital."

"But you can't … I mean, they won't …" stuttered Luke. He didn't know how to explain that his parents didn't believe in hospitals and doctors.

A fireman came up to them. "We've got her out," he said. "They're taking her to the ambulance now."

The police-woman grabbed Luke's arm and ran with him to the ambulance, helping him inside as the doors closed and the siren started.

Luke looked at his sister, pale, silent and still, with an oxygen mask over her face and a drip in one arm. Part of him was glad that someone was trying to save Anna's life, but he had never gone against his mother and father before, and he knew they wouldn't approve.

"My parents ..." Luke began.

The ambulance man interrupted Luke before he could say that the medical teams had already done too much. "Don't worry, son, we'll find them."

Luke said nothing, but inside he was worrying about just that. They would find his parents, and his parents would be really angry. This was the first real test of what they had taught him to believe, and he was failing it.

The crowd around the crash scene was growing bigger – too big for the police to control. The ambulance began to make its way between the people. It drove slowly, trying not to jog Anna too much.

"Back, everyone! Back!" shouted a police-man. "And put that fag out. Can't you smell the petrol? You're putting us all in danger."

A group of girls had been smoking in the bus shelter when the crash happened. One of them dropped her cigarette down on to the pavement, ready to stub it out with her foot. But it caught a trickle of petrol from one of the cars. There was a whoosh and a ball of flame. The ambulance driver put his foot down, and they sped away. Through the window in the back door, Luke could see an orange glow from a burning car behind them.

He and Anna were safe. They had got out just in time. So why was Luke so worried that he would be in trouble when his parents found them at the hospital?

Chapter 3
Belief

Luke's parents had always been a little different. Until Luke was about ten that had just meant brown bread sandwiches in his lunchbox, some annoying wind chimes in the garden, and not being allowed to watch adverts on the TV.

Then they had met Pastor David, and started going to the Church of the Healer's Message. Now Luke and Anna had been taken away from school, and the TV was used only for playing DVDs and videos given to them by Pastor David. They were films of church services in America where sick people were healed. They told of their years of agony, and then rose from their wheel-chairs in joy after being touched by the minister.

All the programmes had the same message. True Believers would be healed. Miracles happened. It was just a matter of faith. Illness was sent to punish our sins and the sins of our ancestors.

Luke and Anna had watched those DVDs every day for years. They knew the chanting by heart.

"Oh, Lord, heal me."

"I am not worthy. Lord save me."

"Punish me, O Lord."

At the end of each film, the man who had done the healing made an appeal for money. "Sinners," he said, staring into the camera. "Sinners. I know you are sinners. God knows you are sinners. For he sends you illness and pain when you do wrong."

The audience on the film shouted, "Yes, Lord, we are sinners," and, in front of the TV at Luke's house, his family joined in.

The man on the TV spoke again. "Sinners. Do not give your money to doctors. They cannot really make you better. Give it to the Lord. Send your money to me, here at the Church of the Healer's Message, and I will pray for you. You are sinners. But you are special."

An address in Texas flashed up on the screen. Pastor David had explained that there was no need for Luke's parents to go to the trouble of sending money abroad. They could give it to him, and he would make sure that it reached America. So Luke's parents handed money over every week, and they did what they were told. They kept away from doctors, and trusted in the power of the Lord to heal.

"We are sinners, but we are special," they said, as they wrote the cheques.

So far, all that had meant for Luke and Anna was that they didn't get injections, and they never had to go to the dentist. They'd had coughs and colds, but those went with time, and without medicine. Neither of them had ever had a bad illness. Their parents took this as a sign that God wanted to reward their faith.

But now Anna and Luke were in an ambulance. And both of them were bleeding.

Chapter 4
Bleeding

When they reached the hospital, the staff were running round moving in extra beds. They had heard about the explosion at the crash site, and expected lots of casualties. Luke wanted to stay with Anna, but one of the nurses saw the cut on his hand, and took him into a cubicle to have it cleaned up.

"Please don't put anything on it," said Luke, afraid that his mother would be angry if the nurse used an antiseptic.

The nurse thought he was just being a wimp. "Now don't be silly," she said. "It will just sting a little. There's people far worse off than you. Think of your poor sister, she might need an operation, poor love."

"No," said Luke. "She can't. She mustn't be cut by doctors."

The nurse didn't understand. "They'll do what they have to," she said, as she put a bandage on Luke's hand. "A few scars are a small price to pay for a saved life."

Luke wanted to explain that he was worried about much more than that, when he heard his father's voice. He was shouting.

"How dare you operate without asking us first?"

A doctor replied, "We had no choice. It was an emergency. She had to go to surgery. We had no way of getting in touch with you."

Luke's father was still angry. "Well, get her out of surgery now! We need to see her. We need to pray for her."

"We can't stop the operation," said the doctor. "She'll be in there for a few hours. You can see your son, though."

Now Luke heard his mother speaking. "Our son?" She sounded confused. "But he's at home."

The doctor showed Luke's parents to the cubicle where Luke was being treated.

"What are you doing here?" were the first angry words Luke's father said.

"I cut my hand," said Luke. "I had to smash a window to get to Anna. Sorry."

"Sorry!" shouted his father. "You bet you'll be sorry. Do you mean to say you were here and you didn't stop them attacking Anna?"

"Dad, they're not really attacking her. They're helping her. She might die."

Luke's father only grew more angry. "Yes, she might die," he said. "Can't you see that's what we're worried about? She might die putting her trust in doctors instead of in the Lord! How can the Lord send a miracle if we don't give him a chance?"

The doctor was getting angry too, but trying not to show it. "Perhaps God sent doctors to help," he said, hoping to calm Luke's father down.

"I've heard that argument before," said Luke's dad, and he started repeating things from the DVDs.

As Luke listened to his father and the doctor, he couldn't decide whose side he was on. Every point his father made fitted in with what Pastor David said. There was no need to trust modern medicine just because everybody else did. But the doctor sounded kind.

What if Luke's parents were wrong? Luke had never allowed himself to think that before.

A nurse put her head round the curtain. "We need this cubicle," she said, "We're getting more victims in from the accident. Some of them have nasty burns."

Luke and his parents were moved into a side room to wait for news of Anna. Luke's father was still furious.

"Have you got any change?" he asked Luke's mother. "I'm going to ring Pastor David. He'll know what to do."

Chapter 5
Pastor David

Pastor David arrived a couple of hours later, dressed in the robes he wore in church.

"I've phoned Texas," he said. "The time difference means they have the whole day ahead of them to pray for Anna. And I'll get the word out to our congregation here. Anna will have prayers round the clock."

"We are indeed blessed," said Luke's mother, going down onto her knees and kissing the hem of Pastor David's gown. "I'm so sorry that Anna's here, Pastor David. We would have come to you with her. Luke let us down."

The pastor turned to Luke and stroked the bandage on his hand. "I see Luke has been punished for his mistake," he said.

There was a knock on the door, and a doctor came in. She looked worn out.

"I'm Dr Morris," she said. "I operated on Anna. She hasn't come round yet. But you can sit with her for a few minutes."

Everyone stood up. The doctor turned to Pastor David, to let him know that he should wait behind. "Just the family, for now, sir," she said.

"We won't go in without Pastor David," said Luke's father. "If it's a question of numbers, Luke can stay here."

"But Dad!" said Luke. "I want to see Anna."

Luke's father was angry again. "You've no right to come. We've got to rescue her from the harm you've already done." He turned to the doctor. "Dr Morris, take us to our daughter. Pastor David is coming too."

The tired doctor gave in. On such a busy night she had no time to argue. The three adults followed her out of the room, leaving Luke behind.

Chapter 6
Waiting

Luke waited in the hospital side room. As the hours passed, the relatives of other patients came in. All of them were worried. Some of them were crying. Everybody was talking about the crash, but no one seemed to have seen it happen.

The taxi driver said he had come round the corner and found the white van speeding towards him. The van driver was dead, and couldn't say why he had driven onto the wrong side of the road. The lorry had tried to avoid the van and the taxi, and had hit the parked cars, which had forced the Mini on top of Anna. But what had happened to make the van swerve across the road in the first place? Everyone wanted to know, some people had ideas, but no one had any definite information.

From time to time doctors or nurses came into the room and took families off to see their loved ones. No one came for Luke. Now and then he opened the door a little, and caught sight of the chaos in the emergency unit outside. He saw a film crew being thrown out by security men. He saw people bleeding, and doctors and nurses rushing around. They seemed to have forgotten all about him, and they looked too busy to interrupt. He wanted to ask them how Anna was, and if he could go and see her, but he was too scared to make a fuss.

So he was relieved when a kind-looking lady came in and started talking to him.

"Hello. My name's Janet," she said, in a very friendly way. "What are you doing in here on your own?"

"My sister was hurt in the accident," said Luke. "My parents are with her now."

Janet saw his bandage. "It looks as if you were there too," she said.

"Not really," said Luke. "I got there afterwards. Anna was trapped under a car."

Janet was very interested in that. She kept talking, and asking more and more questions. Before he knew it, Luke had told her their names, their ages, where they lived, and a little bit about their special church. Janet seemed to have a way of getting him to say things without thinking first. Still, he was glad to have someone to talk to, after so long on his own.

"Mum and Dad have been with Anna for ages," he told her. "I'm really worried. No one has told me what's going on."

"I'll help you find out, if you like," said Janet. "I'll find someone to ask. Now, don't you worry."

She gave him a little hug, and just at that moment the door opened, and the police-woman from the crash scene came into the room. She went across to Janet. "Are you looking after Luke?" she asked.

Luke was surprised to hear Janet say that she was, even though they had met only a few minutes before.

"Would you mind if I ask him a few questions?" said the police-woman. "You can stay with him, of course."

So Janet sat with Luke while he told the police-woman everything he could remember about the crash. "I'm sorry I can't be more helpful," he said. "I didn't see it happen. I only heard the noise."

"It's possible that Anna is the only person who saw the crash," said the police-woman. "She may be the only one who can tell us why the van swerved. But I'm afraid she's still very poorly. We can't ask her yet."

Luke was glad when Janet said what he was thinking. "Do you think Luke could see Anna now?" she asked. "He's waited a very long time, and he's quite upset."

"I'll see what I can do," said the police-woman. "Come with me." And Luke and Janet followed her through corridors and into a lift.

As the lift doors opened on the fifth floor, they could hear chanting, and a single female voice shouting, "Please, ladies and gentlemen, I beg you. Let us through. We have to do our jobs!"

Chapter 7
Watching

When they stepped out of the lift they found out what the fuss was about. Pastor David had called the congregation of the Church of the Healer's Message to the hospital to join in prayers for Anna. They were all crammed in the side room where Anna was lying. They were blocking the door, so the medical staff couldn't get in or out. Luke stood on tiptoe, but he couldn't see Anna, only Pastor David leaning over her bed, leading the songs and prayers.

Dr Morris was relieved to see the police-woman in her uniform. "These people are in the way," she said. "They are blocking us. They don't approve of medicine, and they are stopping us from treating this child."

"I'll do what I can," said the police-woman. She started trying to talk the congregation into leaving Anna's room, but no one took any notice. "May I speak to the parents?" she asked.

A man on the edge of the group broke off from chanting and turned round to face the police-woman. He spoke sharply. "They are praying for their daughter. They can't stop. Please leave."

Dr Morris was furious. "The child needs medical help," she said. "You must let us in."

"The child has God's help," said the man. "She is in the Lord's hands. If you don't want her here, we'll take her away."

"You can't do that," said Dr Morris. "Now she's in this hospital we have a duty to care for her." And she tried to push her way past the man.

Pastor David's voice boomed from beside Anna's bed. "Link arms, my children. Hold firm," he shouted, and the men and women of the Church of the Healer's Message made themselves into a human chain around Anna, so that no one could get through.

Dr Morris turned to the police-woman, Luke and Janet. "Come into the office," she said. "We have to work out what to do."

They closed the office door to cut down the sound of the chanting. Dr Morris asked Luke to explain the beliefs of Pastor David's church.

"We believe in the power of the Lord to heal," he said, repeating sayings he had learned from the DVDs. "Medicine is Man's mistake. Doctors are demons sent by the Devil. Medicine masks miracles."

He felt awkward, saying these things to non-believers for the first time. After what he had seen in the hospital that night, he was even beginning to wonder whether what his parents said was true.

"Should I send for more officers?" asked the police-woman. "If there were enough of us, we could throw those people out."

Dr Morris knew that wouldn't work. "There must be at least 20 people in there. We'd probably need two policemen to move each of them. This is a hospital," she said. "We can't fill it with riot police and disturb all the other patients. And what if they do as that man said, and insist on taking Anna away with them? We can't risk her being moved now, while she's so weak."

Janet asked, "Can you keep Anna here if her parents don't want you to? Don't they have the right to take her away?"

"We may have to go to court to decide on that," said Dr Morris. "I'm pretty sure a judge would decide in our favour. But that will take time, and it's already very late."

Janet looked at her watch. She seemed surprised. "Excuse me," she said. "I have to ..." She paused, and looked around her. "I just need to go to the loo. Luke will be OK with you for a little while, won't he? I'll be back soon." And she dashed out of the office.

Chapter 8
The Plan

Janet was gone for a long time. While she was away, Dr Morris and the police-woman made phone calls to their bosses. Luke spent the time trying to solve the problem and wondering whose side he was on. He recognised the chants and hymns coming from Anna's room. "Leave Life to the Lord," they were singing now.

He wanted to believe them. He wanted to think that God would send a miracle and make Anna better without any drugs, tubes, or drips. But he could hear what Dr Morris was saying on the phone. She said Anna had to be watched all the time, and that more treatment might be needed at any moment. There was talk of waking up a judge so that Anna could legally be kept in the hospital's care.

When Dr Morris put the phone down, Luke plucked up the courage to ask, "Could Anna die?"

The slight pause before the doctor spoke told him the answer.

"She may be in danger, yes," said Dr Morris. "But if we can get in to look after her properly, she should recover well. Is there any way you could get your mother to come out, so I can talk to her?"

Despite the words of the hymns he knew so well, Luke believed that the doctors wanted to help Anna. He didn't want to upset his parents, but he couldn't see anything wrong with letting someone check on Anna, to make sure that she was not getting worse. "I'll try," he said. "The congregation know me. They'll let me in."

He went into the corridor, quietly joining in the chant. Then, without making a fuss, smiling as he pushed his way through, he reached his mother's side. She was on her knees by the bed, stroking Anna's hair. Anna lay pale and still, but Luke was glad to see that her chest was slowly rising and falling. She was breathing.

Luke bent down to whisper in his mother's ear. She carried on chanting as he spoke.

"Mum, you must come," he said. "Dad and the others can stay here. I need you outside."

His mother hissed back, "I can't leave Anna. You know that."

"But Mum," said Luke. "You have to come. It's the doctors. They want to ..."

Luke's mother suddenly took more notice. Luke pointed to his bandage, and carried on: "They want to do an operation on my hand."

Luke's mother jumped up, pushing her way through the crowd and pulling Luke after her. The chanting stopped for a moment, and Luke's father rose from his place by the bed.

"No. Stay here. Carry on," said Luke's mother. "Look after Anna. I'll deal with this."

A moment later she was in the office, shouting at Dr Morris.

"I will not let you operate on my son!" she yelled.

"I am happy to discuss that with you," said Dr Morris, who had never wanted to operate on Luke anyway. "But in the meantime, and while you are away from your daughter's bed, I would like a nurse to go in to make sure that Anna is OK."

"Absolutely not," said Luke's mother. "I'm going back to her. Luke, you come with me." She grabbed his injured hand and dragged him back. Now the congregation were praying for Luke's recovery, as well as his sister's.

His plan had failed, and now he was trapped in Anna's room.

Chapter 9
The Early Hours

Everyone was tired. Even Pastor David and his followers. The chanting grew softer, and they took it in turns to catch a quick nap – always making sure that enough of them were awake to stop the doctors getting to Anna. No one dared leave her room, so they had to pee in the sink by the window. They could drink from the tap, but some of them were starting to get hungry.

In the office, Janet made herself useful by getting everybody food and coffee from the hospital canteen. Dr Morris turned on the TV in the corner of the room to try to keep herself awake.

The news channel was running pictures of the crash the night before. They had reporters outside the hospital, interviews with some of the victims, and family photographs of the dead driver of the white van. Still no one knew what had made him swerve and set off the chain of events that had led to disaster. The news-readers were beginning to get bored with the story, hoping for a new head-line.

But then things changed. Dr Morris was horrified to hear her own name come from the TV, as the presenters held up the early copies of the morning papers. A sign saying *Breaking News* flashed on the screen.

"The *Daily Post* has an exclusive from inside the hospital," said one newsreader. "It seems that a group of religious fanatics are holding one of the victims hostage inside the hospital."

The second presenter picked up the story. "The patient is a 13-year-old girl, badly injured in the crash and still unconscious. Police think she may be the only witness to what really happened. Her parents believe a miracle will save her, and they won't let the doctors go near her."

"Where did they get all that information?" said Dr Morris. "We're the only people who know. Who told the *Daily Post*?"

Hospital bosses arrived. "We've got a real problem," said one, as if Dr Morris didn't know. "We've already got news crews here because of the crash. Now they want someone to talk about this mess. And even if we get the court order to keep Anna, the cameras will see us throwing out the protestors. Pushing around religious people. It's not going to be pretty."

On the TV, the news presenters looked more excited now. The sign behind them had changed from *Fatal Fireball* to *Hospital Hostage*.

"At least they're not watching this in there," said the police-woman, nodding towards Anna's room. She couldn't know that Pastor David, taking a break from chanting, was sitting by Anna's bed with head-phones on, listening to the news on the radio.

Chapter 10
Back-Up

Pastor David rummaged under his robes, and pulled a mobile phone from his trouser pocket. He was calling up more supporters. He wanted them to stand outside the hospital, to demand that God should be allowed to cure Anna without help from Man. Most of his congregation were around him in Anna's room, so there weren't many people to do it. But he told the new arrivals to make sure that the news crews filmed them, in the hope that viewers who had never even heard of the Church of the Healer's Message would see them there and come along to join in.

It worked. Before long the sound of a new chant was rising up from outside. People stood with candles, gazing up at Anna's room. By day-break, some people had even made banners. 'Give God a Chance' said one. 'Hands off Anna' read another.

Pastor David went to the window, and looked down on the protest. "This could be great for us," he said to Luke's mother, who was waking from a very uncomfortable nap. He told her all about the newspaper article, as reported on the radio.

"Everyone's talking about us. It's a real chance to get our message across. We must think of a way of getting me out of here to go on TV. We have a chance to win new members of our church – to get more support."

Luke overheard the conversation. He asked Pastor David to tell him more about what the newspaper had said. It sounded as if there was only one place the paper could have got so much information about Anna, her family, and the trouble at the hospital. Janet.

She must be a reporter. All that kindness had been a trick. She had been after a story. And that long trip to the loo the night before had really been a chance to phone her news desk. He was angry with Janet – but even so, he saw that there might be a chance of getting a nurse in to Anna now.

"When I was in the office," he said to Pastor David, "I heard them talking about the crash. They don't know how it happened. Why don't you ask to go on TV to make an appeal for witnesses? They might agree if you offer to let them send a nurse in here – just to look at Anna, not to treat her."

Luke's mother snapped back at him. "Don't be stupid, Luke, we can't abandon our beliefs like that," she said.

But Pastor David didn't agree with her. "No," he said. "I like Luke's idea. I need to talk to someone from the hospital. You know those people, Luke. You go out, and tell them I want to be on TV."

So Luke was allowed back through the blockade of worshippers and into the office again. He frowned at Janet, but didn't say anything in front of the others – and he passed on Pastor David's message.

At first, it looked as if he had failed again.

"I won't give that man a chance to talk to the public," said Dr Morris firmly.

But the police-woman thought it might be worth a try. "We do need to appeal for witnesses," she said. "It's important that we find out what caused the crash. If you don't want to let Pastor David on TV, why not ask Luke's mum to do it – so long as they let a nurse in there in return?"

And so Luke was sent back to get his mother, and she was taken down to the hospital canteen, where reporters from all over the country were setting up cameras and microphones, ready to hear the latest from the police on the crash and Anna, the hostage.

They weren't surprised to see Luke's mother looked tired and upset as she talked about her daughter's injuries. As arranged, she begged anyone who knew the cause of the crash to come forward. But then a reporter asked her a question about the Church of the Healer's Message, and before anyone could stop her she had given out the address of their website, made an appeal for money, and stated her belief in the power of faith to heal without doctors.

By the time the lunch-time news was on, no one was interested in who had caused the crash. Everyone was talking about miracle cures, and whether Anna's parents should be allowed to stop her getting medical care. At the hospital, thanks to the deal which had led to the press conference, a nurse was watching by Anna's bedside. She had gone in with Anna's mother and Luke, after the appeal. But the blockade of believers was still there, keeping the doctors out.

Pastor David was pleased with Luke. He told his parents to stop telling him off. "Luke did well," he said. "He has brought the word of our church to many people. The Lord works in mysterious ways. Maybe God wanted him to bring us here."

It felt good to be praised by Pastor David, and Luke was glad to see his parents smiling at him again. The nurse confirmed that Anna's condition was stable. Luke wondered whether the prayers and songs were working after all. He joined in – glad to be back with his family once more.

Chapter 11
The Ruling

Outside the hospital, the protestors demanding that the doctors should stay away from Anna now faced others who were shouting about her right to medical care. Up in the fifth floor office, the doctors and their bosses waited anxiously for the judge's ruling. They could hear two slogans rising up from outside. 'Make Way for a Miracle,' roared against, 'Let Little Anna Live.'

Then, at half-past two, the call came. The judge had made his decision. Pastor David and his followers must leave the hospital. But

Anna must stay. The doctors must be allowed to treat her.

Dr Morris went to the door of Anna's room, and shouted the news. The chanting stopped for a moment, then a babble of argument broke out, as the congregation gave their views on what to do. Most of them wanted to ignore the ruling and stay put. But Pastor David needed to make contact with his new supporters in the outside world.

"My children!" he shouted, and they fell quiet to listen to him. "You have done well here. You have done God's work. But for now we have been beaten by Man's law. Yet this is not a real defeat. Hear that noise outside."

They all listened to the chanting from the protestors. Pastor David continued. "Let us leave with our heads held high. Let us go out and spread our message. God has sent us this chance."

The congregation looked around the fuggy, smelly room. They were tired. They were ready to go.

"But what about Anna?" said Luke.

He was shocked by his mother's answer. "If Anna must stay here, then we must leave her," she said, staring up at Pastor David. "We must go and do good elsewhere."

Pastor David smartened up his robes, and smoothed down his hair. He told the doctors that the police would not be needed. The followers of the Church of the Healer's Message left in a quiet procession, led by Pastor David. Luke's mother and father came next, walking proudly, with Luke between them. They passed through the main doors of the hospital, singing a hymn about the magic of miracles, to a welcome from their new supporters, broadcast live on TV.

Chapter 11
Victory

Luke's parents protected him from the cameramen and reporters who were shouting his name. The procession stopped briefly, while Pastor David made a speech to the crowd.

"My friends," he said. "Our beloved Anna has been left in the hands of the doctors. We are people of peace. We must obey the law. We have no choice but to leave her. This may seem like a defeat, but with your help, we will turn it into a victory. Join us. Come with us now, and serve the Lord!"

He marched away, and everyone followed, down to the Church of the Healer's Message, which was in a small building by the shopping centre. It had once been a cinema. So many people came that for the first time ever there were not enough seats. It was dark inside, with just a few candles lighting up the crumbling decorations from the days when the hall had been used for showing films. In the dim glow, the fake pillars and swirling designs created a feeling of mystery.

There was singing and chanting, and then Pastor David read out an email from America. The head of the Church of the Healer's Message had seen a report on the day's events on the international news. He praised Pastor David and his supporters, and told them to stand firm against their oppressors. At the climax of the service, Pastor David asked Luke to step forward.

"Hold out your arm!" he ordered.

Luke raised his hand, and Pastor David slowly unwound the bandage, showing everyone the bloody gash made when Luke had climbed through the window, hours ago.

"Behold this wound," cried Pastor David. "It will be healed. I command you all to return, to see how this wound doth heal!" He spat on Luke's hand, and rubbed the spittle into his flesh. It hurt, badly, but Luke tried not to let that show.

At the end of the service there was a collection at the door, and Pastor David asked Luke to stay behind to help him count the money. They had raised nearly £1,000. Pastor David took Luke upstairs to lock it in a heavy safe.

The safe was in what had once been the cinema manager's office. It was a shabby room, next to the Gents' toilets. A sofa bed with rumpled sheets took up most of the room. There was a tiny cooker in one corner, with a saucepan of dried-up baked beans on top. The only chair was piled with dirty clothes.

"Do you live here?" asked Luke.

"Yes," said Pastor David, looking round at the filthy room. "I have humble needs."

****

For the next two weeks, Luke's parents made him visit the Church of the Healer's Message every day. They didn't seem to care about his exams any more.

"You are needed for greater things," said his mother. "Pastor David wants to keep you near him, to work with him at the church."

The TV and newspaper coverage had brought lots of letters, many of them with money inside, and Pastor David needed help writing replies and counting up the cheques. Whenever there was a service, Luke's cut hand was displayed. It healed well, and the congregation took that as a sign that Pastor David's message was true. In the dark of the church, Luke enjoyed being the centre of attention.

Pastor David hardly ever talked about Anna. When he did, it was with regret. The court order banned all the protestors from going anywhere near the hospital. Luke's parents checked on her condition by phone, but it hadn't changed. She was alive but still unconscious. They spoke of Anna as a victim of the doctors.

"Pity that young girl," said Pastor David to the congregation. "She has lost her chance of a miracle. She has been touched by evil now. We must stay away and leave her to her fate."

Everyone focused on Luke and his healing hand.

****

After the evening services, Luke and his parents walked home across town, taking the route his parents had used on the night of the crash. Each time there were fewer signs of the tragic events in Barton Road. The damaged cars and the broken street-light had all been removed. But there was a mark on the tarmac where the fire had burned, and the window Luke had smashed to get out was still boarded up, waiting to be mended.

It all reminded him of Anna, and Luke desperately wanted to see her, even though his parents and Pastor David had told him not to go near the hospital. Nothing had changed at home. The telephone hand-set was still locked in the cabinet, so Luke couldn't even ring the ward to find out for himself how she was, and whether she was likely to get better.

****

Then, one day, when Luke and Pastor David were opening the post in his upstairs room,

Pastor David was called downstairs to the church. Luke noticed that he'd left his mobile phone behind. He couldn't help picking it up. He'd never had a mobile of his own, and it took him a while to work out how to turn it on. He found a phone book and looked up the number of the hospital. Terrified that Pastor David would come back and find out what he was doing, he crept next door into the Gents and quietly made a call.

Luke was surprised. He'd thought it would be difficult to get through to the ward. But after he'd said his name, he heard some clicks, and Dr Morris came on the line.

"Luke. How good to hear your voice," she said. "You couldn't have called at a better time. It's Anna. She's awake, and she wants to see you."

"I'm not allowed to come," said Luke. As he said that, he knew that he sounded pathetic. Then he heard Pastor David coming up the stairs. "But I'll try, I'll find a way," he said hurriedly. He switched off the phone and took it back to its place just as Pastor David came in, ready to give Luke a new task.

The pastor had kept all the newspaper reports on the hospital protest. Until now, they had been in a big pile in one corner of the room. Pastor David had bought a scrapbook, and he wanted Luke to cut out and paste in everything about that amazing night. It was interesting work, re-reading the story, even though most of the papers got lots of things wrong.

But Luke couldn't keep his mind on the job. He had to find a way to visit Anna. He knew that he wouldn't be able to fool his parents. If he was going to get to the hospital, he would have to do it at a time when he was supposed to be helping Pastor David. He had to find a way to distract Pastor David for long enough to make the trip.

Chapter 13
The Visit

Luke got his big idea as he began cutting up the *Daily Post*. That was the paper which had broken the news of events at the hospital – the paper Janet was working for when she had pretended to be so friendly. And there was her name on the story:

Exclusive

Hospital Hostage

Cult hold girl, 13, after fire-ball horror crash

By Janet Marsh

He looked for the phone number of the paper, and wrote it down. Pastor David's phone was still there, on the table beside him. Luke opened the newspaper so that it covered the phone, and slipped his hand underneath. A minute later he said he needed to go to the loo.

In the Gents, he called the number and asked for Janet Marsh. He was lucky. She was there. She started bombarding him with questions.

"Never mind that. I need your help," he said, quickly explaining how he wanted to visit Anna in secret. He made Janet promise to phone Pastor David to arrange an interview. Luke would get to the hospital and back while Janet and the pastor were together. She agreed. He went back into the room, and slid the phone back under the newspaper.

A few seconds later it rang. Pastor David answered it. It was Janet Marsh.

****

Janet arrived for the interview first thing next morning. Pastor David showed her into the church, and Luke told him he was going to sort out the post upstairs. Instead, he took the letters with him, to open at Anna's bedside, and rushed out of the back door and off to the hospital.

"You can't stay long," said the nurse. "She's very weak."

"I'll be quick," said Luke, knowing he had to get back before he was missed.

"How are you?" he asked Anna. "I'm sorry, I have to open these letters while we talk. If I don't Pastor David will know I haven't been working."

"What?" said Anna. "What are you talking about?" And Luke realised that she knew nothing of what had been going on while she was unconscious. He tried to explain it all to her, as he took one cheque after another out of the envelopes, and piled them up neatly on the bed.

"What a lot of money!" said Anna. "Who would have thought that awful night could lead to all this."

"Pastor David says it's a kind of miracle – the trouble over you bringing so many new supporters to the church. I'm so sorry, though – that you're being kept in hospital, and that Mum and Dad aren't allowed to visit you. They'd go mad if they knew I was here. They blame me for letting the doctors get hold of you in the first place. But I couldn't help it, Anna. Please forgive me for stopping you being healed by God. I've been lucky. They got me away in time for prayer to save me."

Anna took Luke's hand, and smiled as she looked at the faint scar. "You know, that might have got better anyway," she said. "The doctors have explained what they had to do for

64

me. I'm not so sure that prayer would have been enough, you know."

"But we'll never know, will we?" said Luke. "Still, I'm glad you're getting better. Have the police been to see you? They thought you were the only person who saw what started the crash."

"You're my first visitor," said Anna. "The nurses have told me I was crushed under a car, but all I can remember is waiting opposite the house for Mum and Dad to come home and let me in. Then there was a very fast motorbike. It was really noisy. It was going so fast that a van had to swerve out of the way."

"That's it," said Luke. "That's why the van swerved. Anna, have they told you? The van driver died."

"Oh, the poor man. I didn't know. Well, I'm sure the crash wasn't his fault. It was the bike. It was speeding all over the place."

"Do you remember anything about the bike?" asked Luke.

Anna closed her eyes and tried to remember. "It had big white stripes up the side." She paused and thought again. "And the rider had a yellow crash helmet. But it passed in a flash. I'm sure it didn't stop."

"You must tell the police about it when they come," said Luke. "They might be able to find it on CCTV. I know we don't have cameras in our street, but they might pick it up somewhere else on its journey."

He carried on opening Pastor David's mail. He was rushing to get it done before he had to leave, and wasn't taking much notice of what he was doing.

"Oh, no," he said suddenly. "I shouldn't have opened this one. It's his bank statement. It's private."

Anna looked across at the letter. There were several sheets, each filled with columns

66

of figures on a neat print-out. "My goodness," she said. "I didn't realise you'd raised that much."

Luke read the total. It was nearly half a million pounds. "We haven't. This must be his own money." He stopped. "But hang on. Look at the address." It was a road on the edge of town.

"He can't live there. Houses in that district cost a fortune," said Anna.

"But it's his name on the statement," said Luke. "And yet he told me he lives in that little room above the church. He said he has humble needs."

Anna took the bank statement from Luke and looked at it closely. It showed lots of regular payments of small amounts of money. "I think I can guess what this is," she said. "You know all those cheques that Mum and Dad have given him to send to Texas?"

"Yes, and I bet they're not the only ones who've been handing over money."

"If you ask me," said Anna, "Pastor David has been keeping the money for himself."

Luke felt once again all the worries about the Church of the Healer's Message that had come to him when he had been in the hospital before, listening to Dr Morris talking about his parents and their faith. Now Anna was wondering if their family had been tricked.

He wanted to talk to Anna more, but the nurse came in and told Luke it was time to leave and let Anna get some rest. He knew he must go. He had already stayed longer than he'd meant to. He hoped Janet had managed to keep Pastor David talking while he'd been away.

Chapter 14
Detectives

Luke raced up the back stairs to Pastor David's room. He placed the cheques on the table, and put the bank statement in his pocket. Then he made two mugs of tea, and carried them downstairs.

"I thought you might like a drink, you've been talking so long," he said.

"Thank you, Luke," said Pastor David, who didn't seem to suspect anything.

Janet gave Luke a look that told him she'd had to listen to Pastor David for far longer than she would have liked.

Luke spoke again. He had a plan for telling Janet about Pastor David and the money. "I wonder if Miss Marsh would like a look at my hand?" he said. "I could show her how it has been healed by prayer."

"Good idea," said Pastor David. And Luke sat down with the two of them and showed off his scar. While Pastor David talked, Luke looked hard at Janet, trying to let her know that he had something to tell her. She understood.

"Pastor David," she said, "may I do a quick interview with Luke, to get a bit more colour for my article?"

"Of course," said Pastor David. "You chat here. I'll go and catch up on my work upstairs."

"I left the post on the table," said Luke.

"Good boy. He's such a help. Such a credit to his parents, and to the church," said Pastor David.

As soon as Pastor David had left, Luke got out the bank statement and told Janet what he suspected – that Pastor David was a cheat and had been stealing money from his congregation.

"If you ask me," he said, "Pastor David is only pretending to live here. He's got another house, on the posh side of town."

Janet was ready to believe him. "I don't like your Pastor David one bit," she said. "I'll wait for you outside in my car later. I don't care how strict your parents are, you're not going home from here when you finish work tonight. You're coming with me to check out this address. And keep your head down – we'll pass by your house on the way."

Chapter 15
The Pastor's House

Number 27 Oakgrove Road was a huge white house with a long drive. Janet and Luke parked across the street and walked up to the front door. There was no reply. They looked to see if there was another way in. All the windows were shut tight.

"It's no good," said Janet. "We can't get in to have a look around. We'll just have to wait and see if Pastor David turns up." She leant against the garage door. It moved a little, tilting upwards, away from the ground. She turned round and gave it a push. It moved some more, then it stopped. "It's not locked properly," she said.

The two of them tried to open the door completely, but it wouldn't budge any further. There was just a little space at the bottom.

"Do you think we could get through there?" asked Luke.

"Come on. Let's try," said Janet, and they struggled under the door. Luke was bigger than Janet, and he tore his shirt on the sharp edge of the metal. He cut his hand again, too.

It was dark in the garage, and after all the effort of getting in there, they were disappointed that it seemed to be empty, with no door through to the house. "Hang on a minute," said Janet. "I'll see if this helps." She turned on her mobile phone, and in the dark, its screen light seemed quite bright. That was when they saw the motorbike leaning against the wall.

It was black, with fat white stripes up the side.

And on the seat was a yellow helmet, just like the one Anna had described.

Luke told Janet what it meant. "Pastor David isn't just a crook. It looks as if he caused the crash."

They squeezed back out from under the garage door and ran to Janet's car. They sat inside, and tried to make sense of what they had seen.

"We shouldn't get too excited," said Luke. "We don't even know if he lives there."

"Oh, come on! It's his name on the bank statement, isn't it?" said Janet.

"And the motorbike? I know it's like the one Anna saw, but I've never seen him riding it. He's always at the church when I arrive first thing in the morning. And he always walks if he needs to go anywhere. We all do. It's part of our simple life."

"Maybe he's keeping the bike hidden. Perhaps he's scared that there was a witness to the crash. Look at the timing. That night, your parents were walking back from church. If he left after the service on a motorbike, he would have passed through your road before them, just about at the time the crash happened."

"And then," said Luke, "when he heard how bad the crash was – when he got a call from my dad at the hospital ..."

"He would have felt bad about not stopping, and left the bike locked up while he went to get Anna away from the doctors."

"He might even have wanted to be with Anna when she woke up, to make sure that she hadn't seen his bike." Luke paused. "Or, worse still, he might have wanted to keep Anna away from medical care to make sure that she ..."

"Never woke up," said Janet. "Maybe he wanted Anna to die. At the very least, he's tried to split Anna off from your parents, so they wouldn't take her side if she gave evidence in court against him. I'm sorry, Luke, but I think your Pastor David is a very nasty piece of work."

As she spoke, Janet looked in her rear-view mirror. A dark figure had turned the corner and was walking towards them. She gave Luke a push and started the engine. "Get down," she said. "It's Pastor David." As she drove away, she kept checking the mirror. "There's your proof," she said. "He turned in to number 27."

"Shouldn't we confront him?" asked Luke.

"No," said Janet. "We're going to the police."

Chapter 16
The Truth

Luke and Janet were talking so fast when they arrived at the police station that the duty officer thought they were wasting his time. But the police-woman from the crash was there and stopped to say hello. She took them into an interview room and gave them a chance to calm down. They told her everything.

"Luke, you'll have to make a statement," she said. "We can't do that without your parents here. I'll help you explain to them what Pastor David has been up to."

"I don't think they'll take it very well," said Luke.

****

He was right. His parents shouted at him for betraying Pastor David, and were livid when they heard that he had visited Anna in hospital. When he'd given his statement, they bundled him out into the corridor to take him home. Two policemen were walking towards them, on either side of a man in handcuffs. His head was slumped, and he looked dejected. It was Pastor David.

Luke's father rushed up to him, gushing with apologies for what Luke had done. "Pastor David! Forgive us. Our son has let you down. Trust us. We will not betray the faith."

Pastor David raised his head and snarled with contempt. "You mug," he said. "You sad, stupid mug."

At that moment, Luke's parents realised that what Luke had said was true. Neither of them spoke on the long walk home, but Luke could feel their anger turning into shame as they realised how their passion for Pastor David had put their children in danger.

When they were safely inside the house, Luke's mother crumpled into tears on the sofa. His father started stuffing Pastor David's DVDs into a bin bag.

Luke felt awful. He could see he had completely destroyed his parents' faith in their church. "I'm sorry," he said, expecting his father to lash out at him again.

But his father started crying too. "No, son. We're the ones who should be sorry. We should never have trusted that man. We've made a big mistake."

Luke tried to comfort his father. It felt odd. "I know, Dad. I know how good it felt to be praised by Pastor David. I know you thought you were doing the right thing. You don't need to apologise to me. But I think you should say sorry to Anna, don't you?"

****

After that, things moved very quickly. The bike was found on CCTV tapes, racing through streets near the crash site. Pastor David confessed to stealing from believers for years. He had never sent money to Texas. He had simply bought some DVDs from the website of a very dodgy church there. Janet Marsh went to America to follow up the story. She won a prize for revealing religious con-men at work in Britain and abroad.

Luke's parents started visiting Anna in hospital, and when she came home, they let her take tablets to ease her pain. They were pleased when Pastor David was sent to prison. But they never got their money back, and they were deeply embarrassed about how they had been tricked. They kept up a proud dignity in public, but sometimes, at night, when they thought the children couldn't hear them, they held each other tight, and sobbed.

The new cut on Luke's hand healed up without help from the church or the hospital, and family life began to change. Luke got his GCSEs. He asked to go to college to do his A-levels, and his parents said yes. He argued, and they agreed, that it was time for more contact with ordinary people, in the real world.

His family were still a little different, but now things were more like the days before they'd joined Pastor David's church. The wind chimes in the garden annoyed the neighbours, and Luke's parents were still strict about TV, clothes and phones. But one way or another Luke and Anna found friends and more or less fitted in.

And they both came to understand that the terrible crash in Barton Road had, for all their family, been a very lucky escape indeed.

Barrington Stoke would like to thank all its readers for commenting on the manuscript before publication and in particular:

Nikki Graham

Ashley Herd

Faye Maidment

Kyle McDermid

Alana Merson

Robert Palmer

Mark Partridge

Catherine Paton

Reece Paul

Adam Porter

J. G. Robertson

Mhairi Shewan

Ryan Stewart

Become a Consultant!

Would you like to give us feedback on our titles before they are published? Contact us at the email address below – we'd love to hear from you!

info@barringtonstoke.co.uk
www.barringtonstoke.co.uk